THE
A-MAZE-ING
FLIGHT TO STRAKKTON™

Vladimir Koziakin

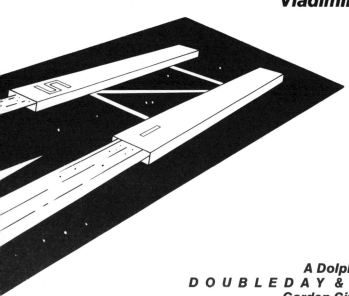

A Dolphin Book
D O U B L E D A Y & C O M P A N Y , I N C .
Garden City, New York
1984

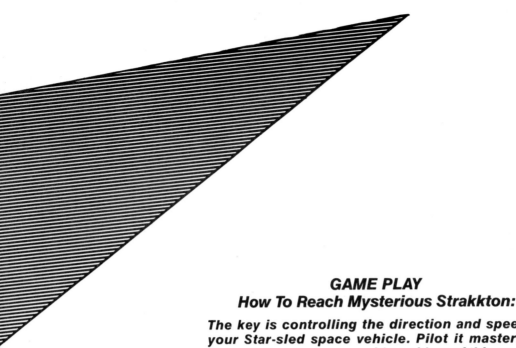

GAME PLAY
How To Reach Mysterious Strakkton:

The key is controlling the direction and speed of your Star-sled space vehicle. Pilot it masterfully through the dangerous grid corridors of this onrushing Cosmic Maze. First, enter the maze section indicated by Star-sled 1 and begin your a-maze-ing journey through space from one Cosmic Maze section to the next. Try and determine as you hurtle through space which correct corridor will propel Star-sled 1 from one maze section to the next. The Cosmic Maze continues from its first page to the last. At times your solution flight will come dangerously close to some of the cosmic pitfalls that appear within the maze. Others may ensnare you and cause time loss. Continue through, Strakkton is getting closer.

HOW TO COMPUTE YOUR SCORE

Each maze section (page spread) has an estimated time for solving. Use the second hand on your watch and keep accurate count of your time, in seconds, for each maze section. Fill in your time in each empty block provided. Occasionally your individual section score will exceed the estimated time. In other sections you will be able to beat the given time. Remember—your total score is the one that counts! At the end of the game play, compute your total time in seconds. Using the age handicaps provided you will be able to attain a final score and match it against the national average chart provided.

Good luck!

ISBN: 0-385-19213-4

The boundless cosmos unfolds. The Star-sled 1, an advanced space vehicle designed to locate and investigate the neo-moon Strakkton is ready for take off. The energy supply of Star-sled 1 is limited and flight speed is the first priority. What dangers will appear to disrupt Star-sled's amazing journey?

EST. TIME: 94 seconds
YOUR TIME:

ALERT: Spacemines swirl in deadly orbits. Keep your space unit on course.

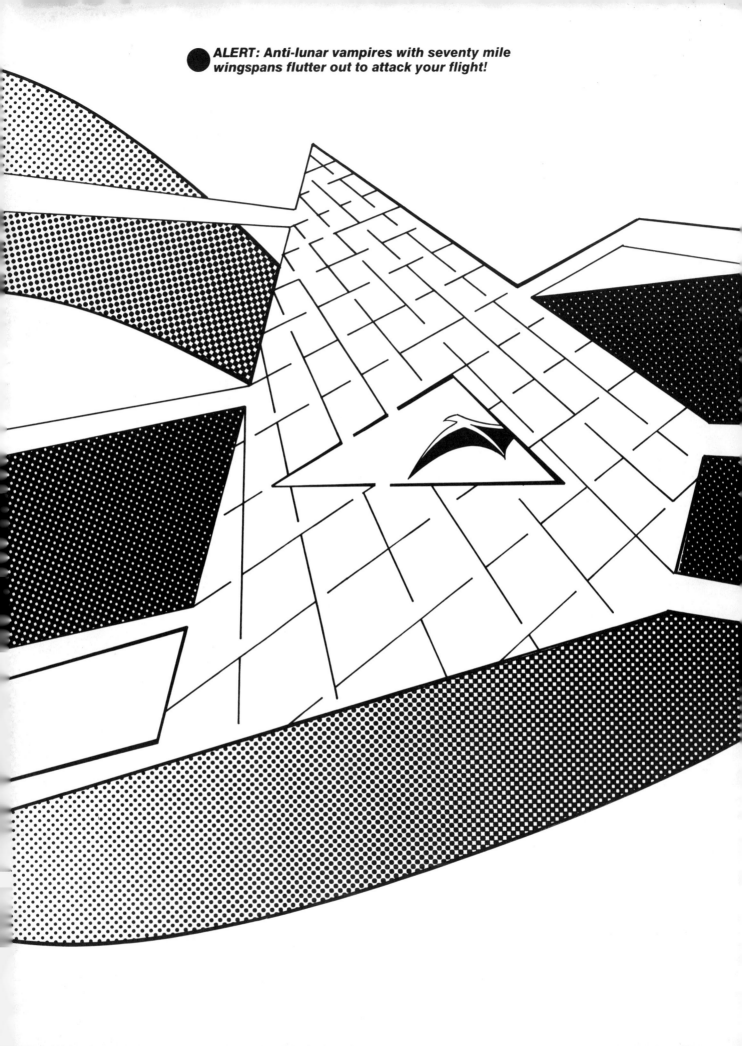

ALERT: Anti-lunar vampires with seventy mile wingspans flutter out to attack your flight!

EST. TIME: 100 seconds
YOUR TIME:

● *A violent electromagnetic storm flashes out to eradicate Star-sled 1. Accelerate!*

EST. TIME: **88 seconds**
YOUR TIME:

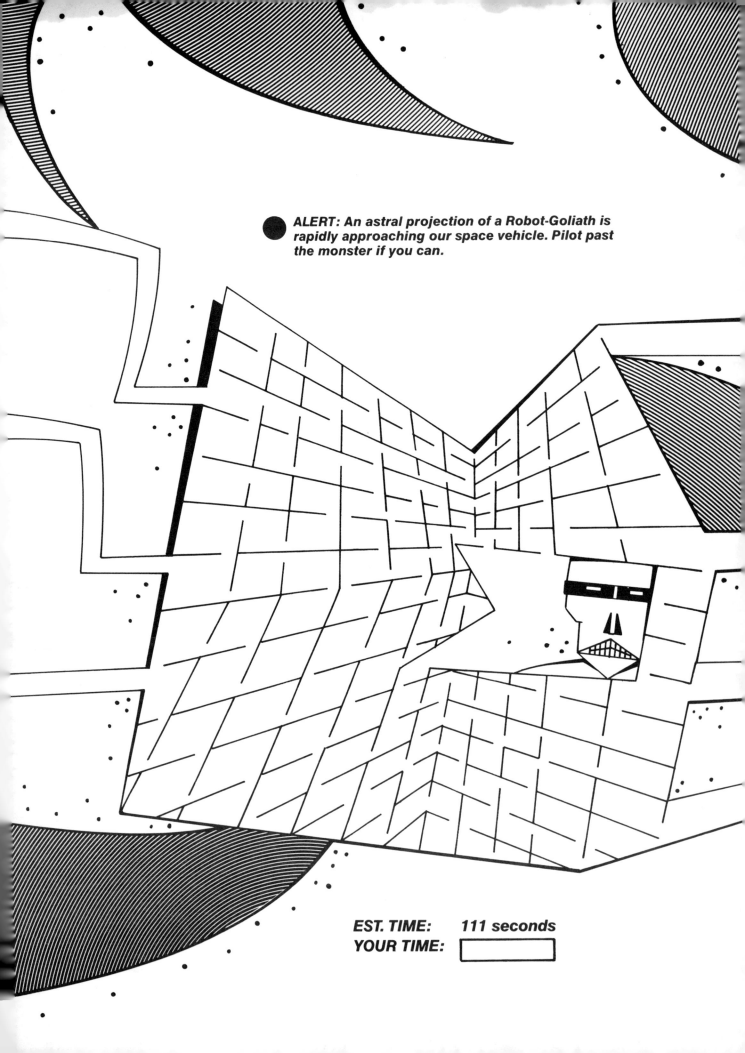

ALERT: An astral projection of a Robot-Goliath is rapidly approaching our space vehicle. Pilot past the monster if you can.

EST. TIME: 111 seconds
YOUR TIME:

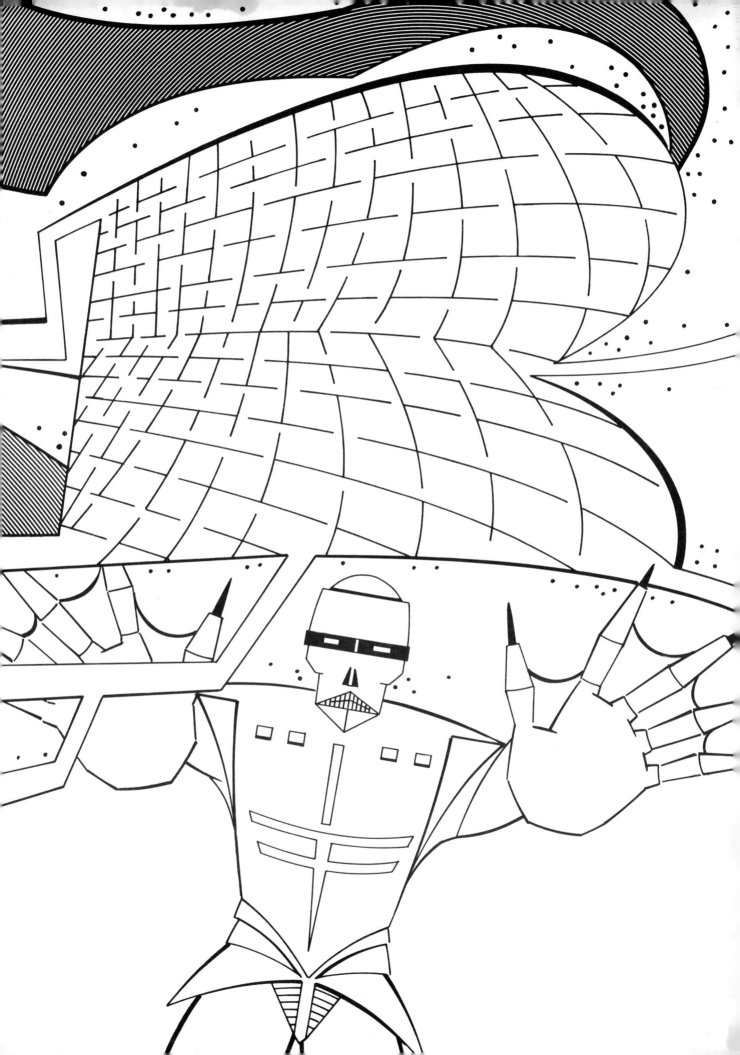

ALERT: Plasti-metallic condors proliferate in this bacterial zone. Proceed with caution.

EST. TIME: 77 seconds
YOUR TIME:

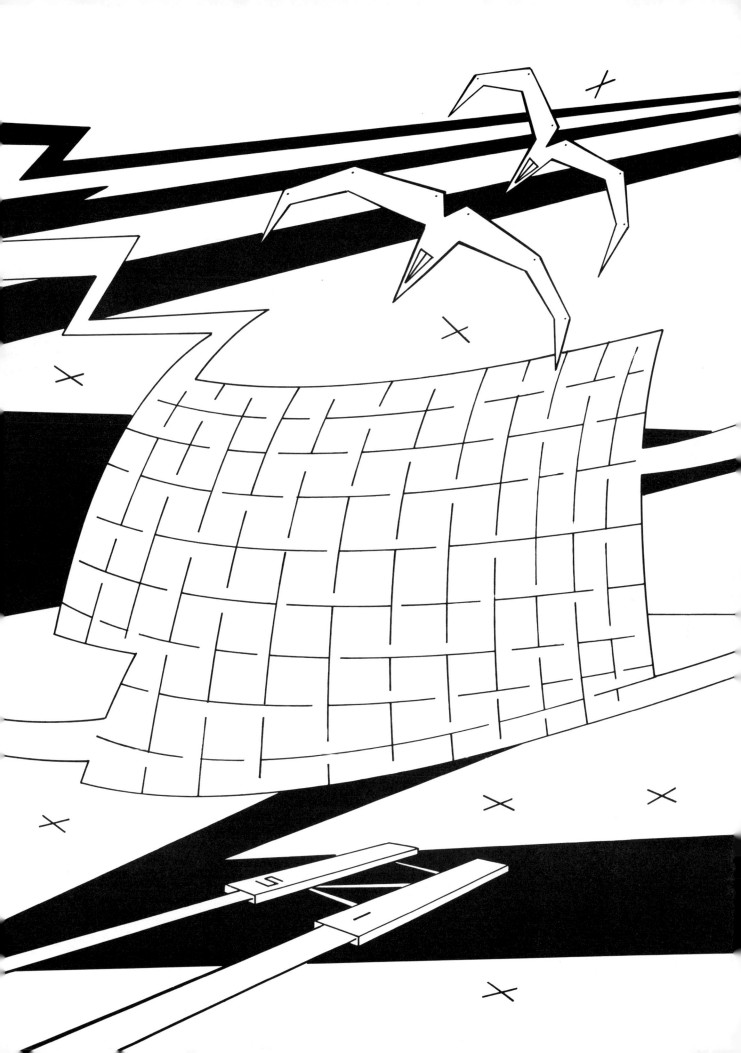

These Scorpion mutations with dioxin-tipped stingers have awaited your arrival for eons.

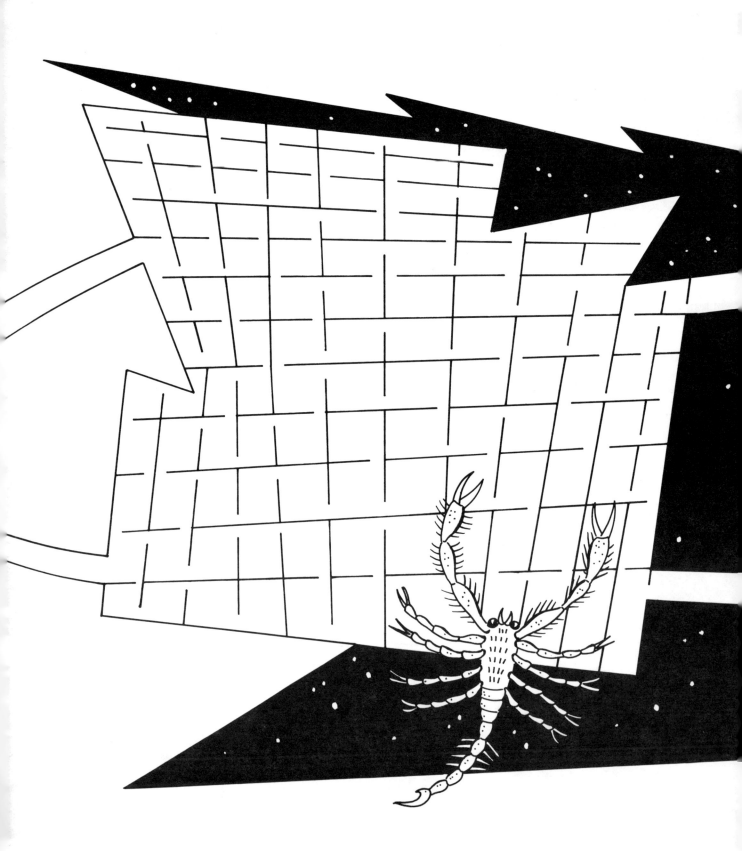

EST. TIME: 68 seconds
YOUR TIME: [   ]

Holographic space flotsam resembling an antique building from Earth materializes to block your flight through this unfurling section of the cosmos.

A carnivorous octopus, larger than an asteroid, poises itself to constrict and destroy Star-sled 1 with its powerful tentacles.

EST. TIME: **10 seconds**
YOUR TIME:

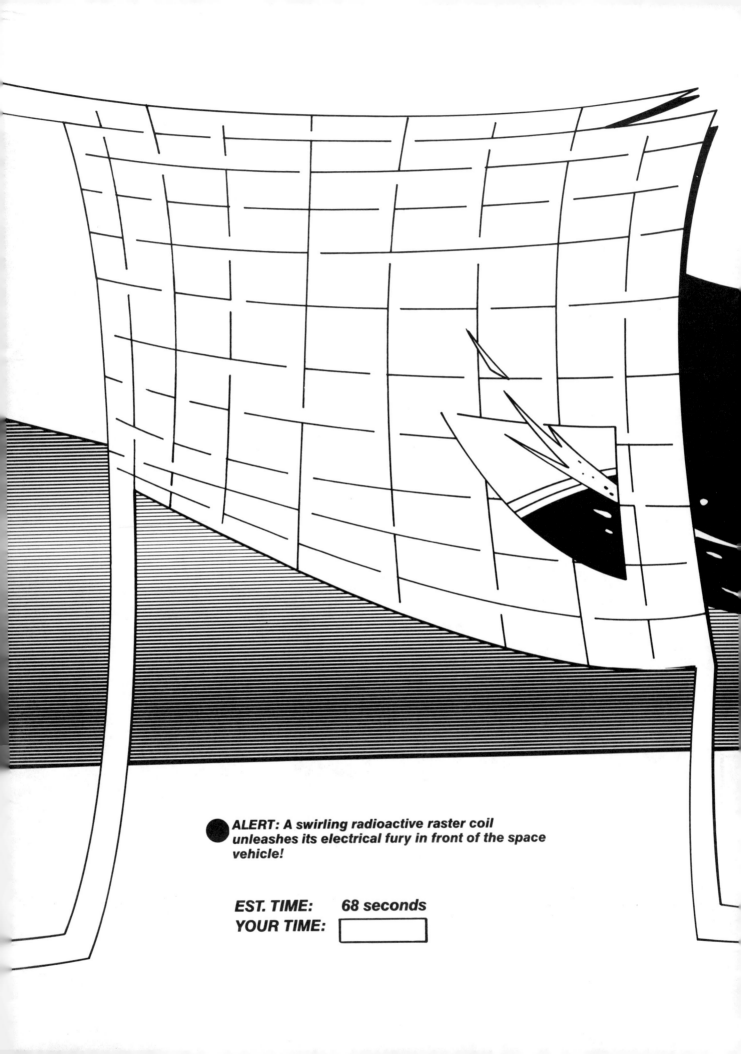

ALERT: A swirling radioactive raster coil unleashes its electrical fury in front of the space vehicle!

EST. TIME: 68 seconds
YOUR TIME:

The deadly serpentine paths of heat seeking warheads cross the flight plan of Star-sled 1 as it nears the indistinct form of the objective— Strakkton! Only seconds remain.

EST. TIME:	79 seconds
YOUR TIME:

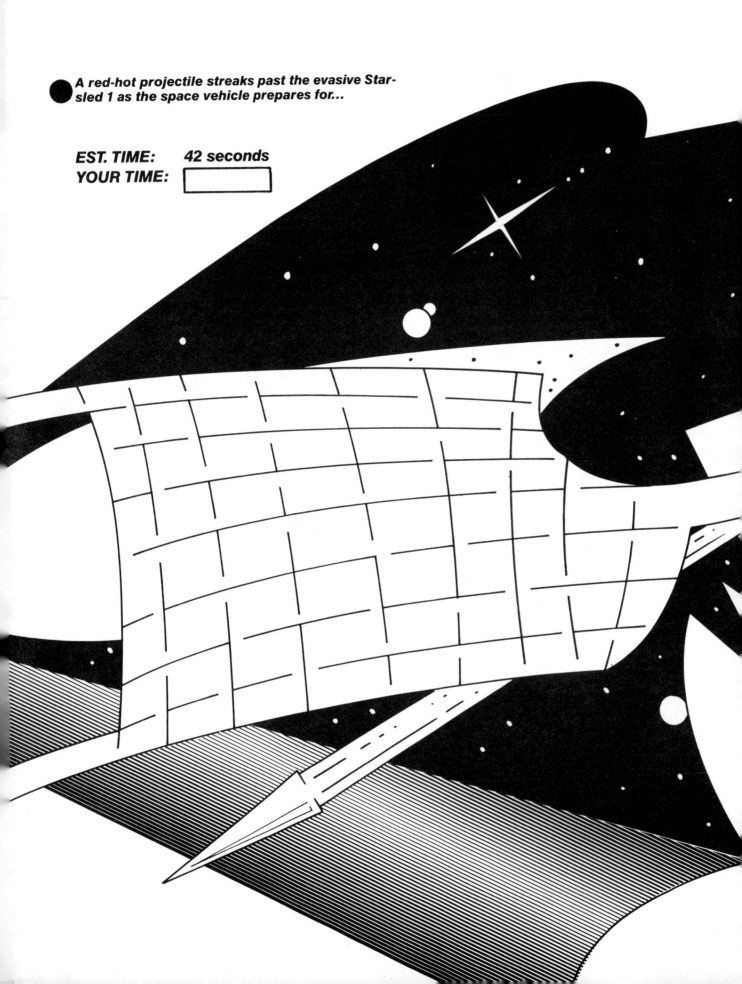

A red-hot projectile streaks past the evasive Star-sled 1 as the space vehicle prepares for...

EST. TIME: 42 seconds
YOUR TIME:

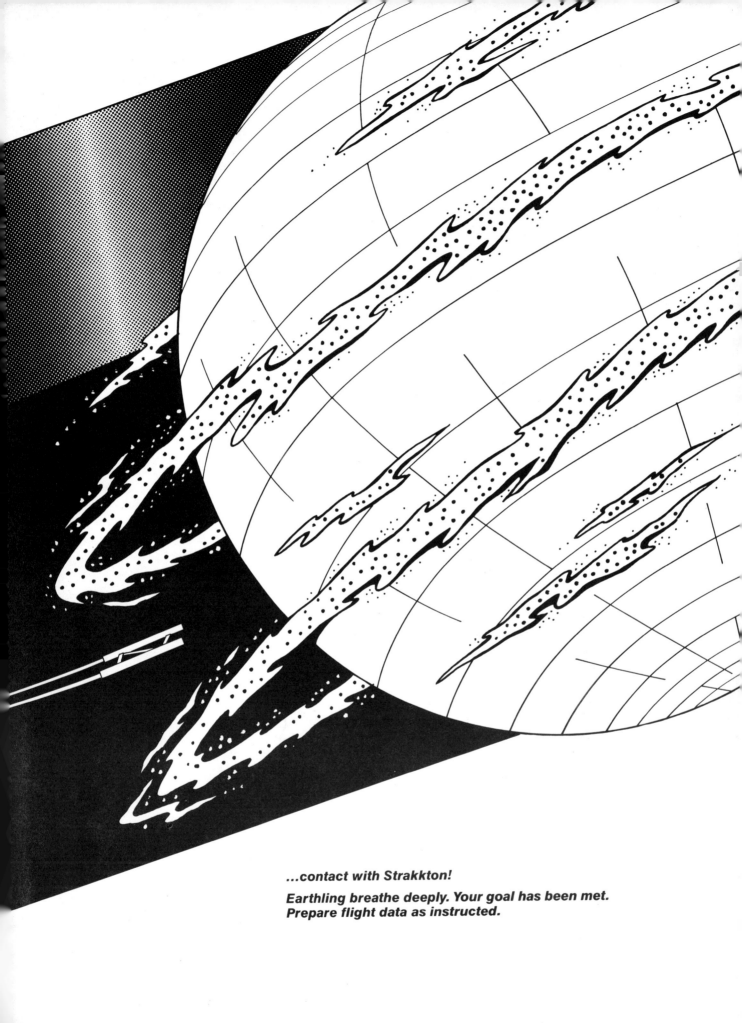

...contact with Strakkton!

Earthling breathe deeply. Your goal has been met.
Prepare flight data as instructed.